For Mauro and the real-life Sam and Sarah
—D. K.

The illustrations in this book were made with Winsor and Newton gouache
on Arches watercolor paper.

Kirk, Daniel.
Library mouse : home sweet home / Daniel Kirk.
p. cm.
Summary: While the library that Sam and his adventurous friend Sarah live in is being renovated, the two mice try to make new homes for themselves in the attic, constructing every-
thing from a yurt to a geodesic dome. Includes photographs of real house styles discussed
and a brief glossary of terms.
ISBN 978-1-4197-0544-1 (alk. paper)
[1. Libraries–Fiction. 2. Dwellings–Fiction. 3. Mice–Fiction.] I. Title.
PZ7.K6339Lih 2013
[E]–dc23
2012039261

Text and illustrations copyright © 2013 Daniel Kirk

Book design by Chad W. Beckerman

Printed and bound in China
10 9 8 7 6 5 4 3 2 1

Abrams Books for Young Readers are available at special discounts when purchased in quan-
tity for premiums and promotions as well as fundraising or educational use. Special editions
can also be created to specification. For details, contact specialsales@abramsbooks.com
or the address below.

ABRAMS
THE ART OF BOOKS SINCE 1949
115 West 18th Street
New York, NY 10011
www.abramsbooks.com

**S**AM WAS A LIBRARY MOUSE. If you were to ask him his favorite things, he would surely say reading and writing. Sam was a storyteller, and a dreamer, and a lover of words.

But if you were to ask Sam's friend Sarah what her favorite things were, she would say exploring and having adventures. Though they had different interests, Sam and Sarah were the best of friends.

One night the two mice were surprised to discover half-empty library shelves and boxes packed with books. Sam's heart was pounding as he climbed up onto the librarian's desk and read the papers he found there. "Renovation," he said warily.

Sarah asked, "What does *that* mean?"

Sam frowned as he went to the dictionary to see what the word meant. "To make new again," he read aloud. "So they're going to redo the library. But it looks perfect to me just the way it is! And if those plans are right, they're going to have to take it all apart before they can fix it. Where will we live while the work is done?"

"The two of us will have to go exploring and find a new home," said Sarah.

In the library kitchen, Sarah led Sam into the dark space beneath the sink. "There's room in here for a couple of mice," she said.

But the sound of running water in the pipes made Sam feel very nervous.

Next, Sam and Sarah crept down to the basement. "Let's keep looking," Sam said with a shudder, eyeing a dusty old mousetrap in the corner.

"What about this?" Sarah said, as they climbed up the creaky stairs to the library attic. "Nobody ever comes up here!"

"I can see why," Sam said, gazing into the shadows. "There's too much space up here for me. I need a home that's a little cozier."

Sarah said, "Then you could build a house right here, Sam, something just your size."

"That's a great idea!" Sam said. "I'm going to build the perfect house for a library mouse."

"And I'll build one, too," Sarah said. "A house for an explorer who has adventures!"

First Sam and Sarah moved all their belongings up to the attic. "I hope they haven't packed up the architecture books yet," Sam said.

"Architecture?" Sarah repeated. "What's that?"

"It's the art of designing buildings," Sam answered. "And somebody who designs buildings is called an architect. Let's get going. We've got a lot of research to do!"

Sam and Sarah went back to the children's room and found the books they were looking for on top of a box. The books were filled with pictures of all types of buildings. "This is the kind of thing I like," Sam said, studying classical buildings from ancient Rome.

"And this looks great to me," Sarah said, looking at a
Mongolian home called a yurt.

The two mice gathered materials from anywhere and everywhere in the library. Then they hauled their supplies up to the attic and began making their new houses.

Building was hard work. Sam used cardboard and tape for the walls, and tubes from paper towel rolls for the columns. When he was finished with his house, he stood back to take a look.

"It's all right," Sam said, "but it just doesn't feel cozy like home."

"I love my yurt," Sarah said.

"This isn't the perfect house for a library mouse," Sam said. "Let's go back down to the children's room. Maybe I'll find something to get me inspired!"

"A castle," Sam said, turning the pages of his book. "You know what they say, a mouse's home is his castle! I don't have any stones, but I saw a package of marshmallows in the kitchen I could use for building."

"Oh, look at this igloo," Sarah said. "I could make one with sugar cubes. And if we get tired of our new houses, we can just eat them!"

Sam and Sarah spent many nights working in the attic. But during the day, when they tried to sleep, the sound of hammers and saws drifted up from the library below.

Finally Sam finished his castle. "It looks very grand," he said, "and I'd feel safe in there. But it just doesn't feel like home."

Sarah said, "You'll always be a library mouse, Sam, no matter what kind of house you live in. But as long as you keep building, I will, too. There are so many kinds of houses to make!"

**Over the next few weeks, Sam built:**

**a cottage with a thatched roof,**

**a Tudor-style house,**

a bungalow,

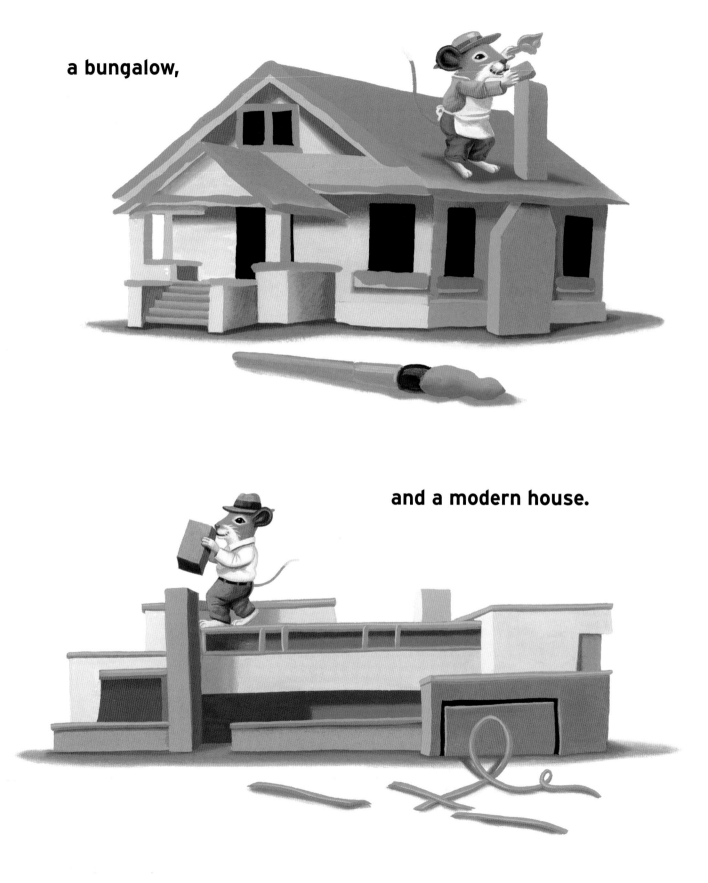

and a modern house.

**Sarah had fun making an acorn-shaped house from Bolivia,**

**an earthen castle from Togo,**

a Vietnamese stilt house,

and a space-age geodesic dome.

"These houses would be nice for somebody," Sam said, "but I haven't found the perfect house for a library mouse."

"Come on," Sarah said. "What's wrong with the ones you built?"

Sam frowned. "I miss my library."

He went back down to the children's room, hoping to look at some more books about architecture. But he found the windows taped over and the door sealed shut.

Sam trudged back up to the attic. He wondered how he would ever feel at home again, like he had in his little hole beneath the children's reference books.

At the top of the stairs, Sarah met her friend with a smile on her face. "Come look at what I made for you, Sam!" she said.

"I found an old book in the corner. It's called an atlas, and it's full of maps! I stood it on end and opened it up, and just like that, I made you an A-frame house, like one I saw in a book."

"Wow!" Sam said, lying on his back and looking up at the map that made the slanting walls of his new home. "It's cozy and pretty close to perfect! Thanks, Sarah."

Sam loved his new house, and he was very happy. But when he tried to go to sleep, he tossed and turned. With a start he realized it was because the library was too quiet—there wasn't any hammering or pounding anymore!

Later that day, Sam went to get Sarah. "I think they finished working on the library," he said. "Lets take a look!"

Sam gasped at the sight of the new, renovated library. It was truly beautiful, and better than ever.

"There's just one thing," Sam said to Sarah.

The next morning, when the children arrived, there was a sign that read, "Home and where to find it." Along the top of the shelves was an array of houses from all over the world.

"They're like the displays we had before!" a child said.

"They make the library feel like home again," said another.

And Sam and Sarah were the first to agree!

# About This Book

Houses are different all over the world. Some houses are built to withstand harsh weather such as snow and ice or flooding rivers. Others are built for people to live in as well as to act as strongholds or forts. Some houses are built as a sign of the wealth and power of the owner, while other houses are simple and modest.

In this book Sam and Sarah build a range of different houses. There are many other types, or styles, of homes to discover as well. Here is a brief description of each of the houses that Sam and Sarah build.

**classical building (Ancient Greece and Rome)** This is the Pantheon in Rome, which in ancient times was considered the home of many gods. It uses columns to support the roof. Today, homes, libraries, and other buildings often mimic this type of architecture. *Photo © r.nagy*

**yurt (Mongolia)** A yurt is a portable house used by nomads in Central Asia. Because its residents move from place to place, the yurt can be taken apart and reassembled at a new site very easily. *Photo © AlenVL*

**castle (Europe)** This is Leeds Castle in Kent, England, built in 1119 and most likely used as a stronghold or fort. By 1278 it was the property of Edward I. He transformed it into a royal residence as well as reinforced its defenses. *Photo © JeniFoto*

**igloo (the Arctic)** Igloos, or snowhouses, were originally built by the Inuit people. Some igloos were built as temporary shelters by hunters and travelers, while others were larger and built to house one or two families. *Photo © Michel Cecconi*

**thatched-roof cottage (international)** A thatched roof is made of dry vegetation such as straw, water reed, sedge, rushes, or heather. Thatched roofs can be found all over the world, and some people even use thatching for the walls, too. *Photo © Lukasz Pajor*

**Tudor-style house (England)** This style originated in the 1500s. A Tudor house has a post-and-beam construction. It is created by joining timbers of wood using large wooden pegs and adding plaster between the timbers. The house has a steeply sloped roof; prominent cross gables (a gable is the triangular section formed by a sloping roof); tall, narrow doors and windows; small window panes; and large chimneys. *Photo © St. Nick*

**bungalow (international)** This is typically a single-story house with an open floor plan and porches. It is built to allow easy airflow and cross-circulation, especially in dry climates. There are many styles; Craftsman and Spanish are two popular types. *Photo © LesPalenik*

**modern house (international)** This is a style marked by simplicity, clean lines, geometric forms, and materials such as wood, metal, and plastic. It emphasizes ample windows, open floor plans, and bringing the outdoors in. *Photo © photobank.ch*

**round or acorn house (Bolivia)** These houses have rounded lines and edges rather than straight ones, because they're built in very windy areas. The curved walls allow the winds to sweep around the house more easily. *Photo © Viaje al corazón de Bolivia*

**earthen castle (Togo)** This house is entered by the large door on the left, while ducks and other animals enter through the small, round door on the right. The people and animals live together on the first floor, but the people go up to the second floor to sleep. *Photo ©*

**stilt house (Vietnam)** Suited to flood-prone plains and steep mountain slopes, a stilt house is made from wood, bamboo, cane, or rattan. The area under the house is sometimes used as a pen for livestock. *Photo © Rungbachduong*

**geodesic dome (international)** Efficient, inexpensive, and durable, these spherelike structures are composed of a complex network of triangles. They can be used as homes as well as for emergency shelter and mobile military housing. *Photo by VisionsofAmerica/Joe Sohm*

**A-frame house (international)** This style features steeply angled sides that usually begin close to the ground and meet at the top of the roof in the shape of the letter *A*. Inside, an A-frame ceiling is open to the top rafters. *Photo © Khoroshunova Olga*

# Glossary

**architect:** a person who designs buildings

**architecture:** the art of designing and constructing buildings

**atlas:** a book of maps

**building:** a structure such as a house, a library, or other enclosed construction, used for a variety of activities

**column:** an upright support, often decorative

**home:** a residence of a person, family, or household that reflects their personality, taste, heritage, or interests

**house:** a building in which people or animals live

**plans:** drawings, often called a blueprint, that show how a room, house, or building will be built, modified, or restored

**renovation:** the act of renewing or updating a house or other building

**research:** to investigate and gather information on a subject